Christmas Eve Casanova

Gwyn McNamee

Christy Anderson

Christmas Eve Casanova
© 2021 Gwyn McNamee & Christy Anderson

All rights reserved. Except as permitted by U.S. Copyright Act of 1976, no part of this publication may be reproduced, distributed, or transmitted in any form or by any means, or stored in a database or retrieval system, without prior permission of the author.

The scanning, uploading, and distribution of this book via the Internet or via other means without the permission of the publisher is illegal and punishable by law. Please purchase only authorized electronic editions and do not participate in or encourage electronic piracy of copyrighted materials.

This book is a work of fiction. Names, characters, establishments, or organizations, and incidents are either products of the author's imagination or are used fictitiously to give a sense of authenticity. Any resemblance to actual persons, living or dead, events, or locales is entirely coincidental

BLURB

Cass A. Nova is a massive dick.
Always has been.
(He also has one, but that's neither here nor there).
My older brother's best friend loved to taunt me and call me Virgin Mary growing up.
He also embarrassed me in the worst way when he found out I was crushing on him.
Now that I'm back in Smalltownsville, I hope I never have to see that smug man again.
Fate seems to have other plans.
All because of the ginormous candy cane in his hand.
It's exactly what I need to fulfill my needs.
Too bad Cass isn't willing to give it up.
But neither am I.
We both want what that girthy minty rod can offer.
So maybe it's time to forget the past and spread my legs to find some holiday cheer, courtesy of my very own Christmas Eve Casanova.

Chapter One

MARY

If there's one thing I can count on now that I'm back in Smalltownsville, Illinois—besides it being freezing cold and snowing on Christmas Eve—it's running into someone I don't want to see.

Case in point—Cass Alexander Nova.

Who names their kid Cass A. Nova, anyway?

Assholes, that's who.

His parents were clearly assholes—at least on the day they named him—and the way he treated me growing up didn't speak very well for their parenting skills, either.

Bobby's best friend was ruthless, smug, condescending, and so, so, *so* hot. It was like watching a scene from *Baywatch* every time he came over to use our pool with big bro. His sandy-blond hair would darken when wet, and he'd climb up the ladder, water trickling over his picture-perfect, golden abs to disappear down over that *V* thing that led to...

Well, I never saw it.

At least, not unencumbered by some sort of restrictive clothing. Like those tight white baseball uniforms...or those damn gray sweatpants Cass always wore that clung to him and left nothing to my sixteen-year-old imagination except what I fantasized about every night while I flicked my bean. Or those jeans that hugged his ass perfectly and showed off just how flawless he was in every way.

The man was a *god* in high school, lofty and worshiped by women *and* men...and four years older than me. Glaring at him now, even a decade later, after we've both grown and matured, I can see not much has changed.

Still hot as hell...and still an asshole.

Just look at him...schmoozing and flirting with that soccer mom in her tight yoga pants and low-cut sweater that exposes her probably fake, too-round breasts. It's too cold to be dressed like that, but her body is probably made of so much silicone that she can't even feel the chill. He doesn't even care that she's bouncing a toddler on her hip. That same sexy smile. The panty-melting laugh. He throws them at her like an archer zeroing in on his target.

Gag!

Even the little one seems entranced by him, too. Bright-blue eyes staring at him with fascination. Giggling and playfully high-fiving with the man who crushed my teenage soul.

Oh, my God! Is that kid giving him a piece of candy?

I squint against the bright late-morning sunlight reflecting off the snow all around to try to get a better look. The little girl reaches out and pushes a piece of chocolate into the mouth Cass has used to seduce probably hundreds of women over the years.

Jesus! The guy is LITERALLY taking candy from a baby!

He's apparently reached even lower lows since I've been gone. Not shocking considering how he acted back then. Silly me for even considering someone might change in a decade.

God knows I have. Ten years away from this place did me good. I got to explore the world...or at least a few parts of it. I got to experience things this tiny speck on the map never could have offered. I grew in ways that would have been stunted had I stayed.

But apparently, all Cass did after he graduated from college was come back here and fall right back into old habits—seducing women and breaking hearts.

And now he's added stealing candy from babies to his asshole resume.

I turn away from him before my blood literally boils out of my ears and make my way down the line of festive Christmas displays. Shopping at the Saturday morning Holiday Market makes my return home finally feel *real*. Even though it's been a week since I set foot back in the city limits, spending all my time at home or at the restaurant means I haven't had a chance to explore and get back to all the things I once loved to do growing up here. And the Holiday Market—held on the Saturday before Christmas, which just happens to be tomorrow this year—has always been one of my favorites.

The colors.

The smells.

The friendly smiles of people who have worked so hard and planned for months and months to be here even in the snow and bitter cold to sell their products in the crisp morning air.

It couldn't have come at a better time, either. There are only a few hours left to get what I need before tonight's massive Christmas party, and Becky is one of the worst clients I've ever worked with, so everything must be *picture-perfect*, especially the white chocolate peppermint cake—that *must* include *handmade* candy cane. Store-bought candy canes just aren't sufficient, at least according to her. *"We need more!"* Because, apparently, Becky had this cake at a friend's party in Chicago last Christmas and insists it's *"the classiest thing she's ever seen"* and that *"she could absolutely taste the difference because they used homemade ones instead of those cheap, sugary pieces of crap most people eat."*

Gag again.

Not that I have anything against white chocolate peppermint cake. In fact, they're quite delicious, but it took everything in me not to roll my eyes when she said that. There was no point in arguing with her or making other suggestions based on the *many* creative things

Bobby and I can make at the restaurant. The woman knows what she wants and won't be swayed.

So...I didn't bother. Just pasted on my practiced, sweet smile and agreed while biting my tongue so hard that I tasted a tinge of coppery blood in my mouth.

But it *had* to be done. This party is too important to blow it over a damn cake—the first one I'll be catering for Sweet Home Kitchen since I came back to help Bobby run the family business. Which is, thankfully, thriving despite this town seemingly being stuck in the 1970s forever. He can't handle it all himself anymore, and somehow, I let him talk me into returning home to head up the catering side.

It felt like a good move at the time, a break from the hustle and bustle of Chicago, a return to a more laid-back and casual life after constantly being on the go and feeling claustrophobic in a city with almost three million people in it.

But after seeing Cass, I'm reminded why I wanted to leave in the first place. Well, at least one of the reasons. Small towns offer no hope for avoiding people from your former life, people who have hurt you and twisted you apart so badly that you never *wanted* to come home until now.

Hopefully, I can keep our run-ins to a minimum, though. With as busy as I anticipate being, it's not like I'll have any time to socialize, and even if I did, he'd be the last person I would choose to spend it with.

I'd much rather enjoy the fresh air and slight breeze—the sights and scents of the holidays. I grab a blood orange from one of the baskets on the table in front of me and bring it to my nose to inhale deeply.

Perfection.

They'll be amazing in my holiday sangria at the party tonight. I throw a few more into my basket and scan Mrs. Beasley's stall for the other things I need. Growing up, she always had the best homemade candies in town, and I'm hoping that's still true.

Dammit. No candy canes.

Hopefully, one of the other stalls has them since Mrs. Beasley's doesn't. I pay her with a smile and wander farther down the line and to the largest stall, operated by Old Jerry Bloom—one with multiple tables covered with dozens of assorted candies and other seasonal items.

Hand-painted red and gold ornaments, twinkling lights, fruit cakes...

He must have been working in his shop all season to have so many beautiful items available. But I can't seem to find the one thing I desperately need...until my eyes land on something beautifully striped.

Aha! A candy cane!

And just my luck...it's a massive one! Long. Girthy. Satiny smooth. It's everything I could ever want in a peppermint stick. My mouth practically waters just looking at it. It will be perfect for the cake and will hopefully appease Becky.

I reach out and wrap my hand around it, but it's so huge, my fingers don't even touch. Jerry always did enjoy making oversized sweets to delight the children, but this is big even by his standards. Shifting forward, I try to get a better grip, but another hand closes around the other end of it and tugs.

What the hell?

Whoever has the other end of this thing better release it.

My gaze drifts up, and I come face to face with my worst fear.

Cass...of fucking course.

His blue eyes twinkle with amusement and that special *thing* he always had, and the corner of his perfectly pink lips curls up into that sexy half-grin that's always made my legs weak. "Well, well, well, if it isn't Virgin Mary Sweet. Bobby mentioned you were back in town to run the catering side of the restaurant."

I scowl at him and secure my grip on my prize while I try to find my composure. This man will *not* see me flustered. I will *not* give him the upper hand. EVER. "What about you, Cass? Still roaming the halls of the high school, seeing how many girls you can get to flash you their boobs?"

He snorts and shakes his head, leaning toward me slightly with a knowing smirk. "You're just mad I never asked you to."

Goddammit. He's not wrong.

I *did* hate that he never asked me to, that he only looked at me as Bobby's little sister. That the four-year age difference between us meant I was always a kid to him. And the memory of the day he shattered all my hopes and dreams and decimated my soul comes flooding back like it was only yesterday instead of half a lifetime ago.

It was my fault, really. I never should've told Karen that I had a crush on him. That filthy bitch never could keep her mouth shut about anything. And how he reacted is forever etched into my brain like a brand. The smirk he cast at me when she told him I was infatuated. The smug way his eyes scanned me from head to foot before he laughed and said, *"You wouldn't know what to do with me, Virgin Mary,"* and then walked away, crushing my heart under his black boots on his way. It left a permanent scar that burns now staring into the eyes I could swim and drown in.

Well, I won't let Cass A. Nova, and his beautiful baby blues drag me down to the depths of lust-induced insanity again. I tighten my hand around the candy cane and jerk it toward me. I won't dignify his comment with a response. "Are you going to let go of that?"

He glances down at the sugary source of our current conflict and raises his pale eyebrows. "Why would *I* let go of it? I was here first. And for the record, the only time I spend at the high school anymore is to help coach the baseball team."

I tug on my intended prize again, but his grip remains firm. "Bullshit. It's mine."

He jerks back just as hard, but if there's one thing "Virgin Mary" has learned over the last ten years, it's how to have a firm grip.

I growl low at him. "I'm sure there are other candy canes. Give me this one."

And then leave me alone and stay the hell out of my life FOREVER!

"Actually, guys, that's the last one."

"What?" We both turn our heads toward Old Jerry, the unfortunate purveyor of the stand and witness to our little tiff.

Cass twists his lips into a scowl. "What do you mean? There aren't any more?"

Jerry shrugs. "It's Christmas Eve. This is the last one. Pretty sure even the grocery store doesn't have any right now."

You have got to be fucking kidding me.

I turn back to Cass and steel myself to throw-down. "You will take this candy cane over my dead body."

Chapter Two

CASS

I'd like to do a lot of things with this candy cane and her body, but it wouldn't be much fun if she were dead. It would actually be a bit creepy, too. Okay, a lot creepy. But Mary Sweet's warm, willing body pressed against mine is quickly becoming my biggest fantasy the longer we argue.

Damn, did the last decade do her good.

Mary as a teenager—and my best friend's younger sister—with her caramel waves and striking amber eyes was cute, but Mary as a full-grown woman, filled with piss and vinegar and a fiery temper that heats and pinkens her pale cheeks...now *this* isn't cute. It's absolutely smoldering hot.

The longer we have this standoff with the long, thick, hard candy, the harder *my* candy cane grows, straining against the unforgiving zipper of my jeans. Mary clearly thinks she will win this war, but she has no idea how determined I can be when I see something I want.

She twists those beautiful bow lips up and huffs. "What do you need the candy cane so bad for, anyway?"

"That's a complicated question, Mary. My plans for it might be changing...but originally, I needed it for my candy cane mojitos at the bar. It's my most popular Christmas drink."

One of her dark eyebrows wings up. "Are you a bartender?"

I chuckle and smirk, inclining my head backward. "I own a bar just down the street, where the mercantile used to be."

She purses her lips together, apparently annoyed I actually *own* a business when she no-doubt thought I'd be some deadbeat loser. "I see. Well, you'll just have to find another type of mojito for tonight because I *need* this."

"What do you *need* this for so badly?" I lean forward until my lips almost brush her ear. A sweet, flowery scent envelops me and stirs my already-hard cock, and I bite back a groan. "Do you have something *private* planned for it this evening?"

Her tiny gasp of indignation makes my dick jump. "How dare you!"

I pull back and grin at her. "That isn't a no."

Anger darkens her eyes, and she places her free hand against my chest and shoves. But a tiny thing like her can't budge me, and I playfully flex my pecs under her palm in response, knowing she can feel it even through the sweater I'm wearing.

"Stop it, Cass! I have a Christmas party to cater tonight. A very important one for the restaurant. And the client was very specific that she wanted a white chocolate peppermint cake."

"Ooooh, fancy!" I waggle my eyebrows, knowing it will set her off again.

She huffs and tugs at it again. "Give it to me!"

Oh, God, how I long to hear her say those words while I'm buried inside her.

I glance down at the huge confection being held tightly on either end—my large, calloused hand on one side, her petite one on the other. "I have an idea that might just give us both what we want."

That pretty scowl returns to her face, looking sexier and poutier than anything else. "Oh, yeah, does it involve you handing over the candy cane and disappearing from my life forever? 'Cause if not, I'm not interested."

"You were very interested back in the day, Virgin Mary." If I knew Bobby's kid sister would grow up to look like this, I'd definitely have been more receptive to her crush.

Mary huffs out a laugh but doesn't deny it. She was always trying to hang around when I was over at their house, but the few years that separated us meant we weren't even remotely on the same level—her tits hadn't even come in the last time I saw her. But they are *definitely* on display now. My height advantage gives me the perfect angle to peek right down the *V* of her sweater, where those perfect globes push up against the soft material. I lick my bottom lip, totally ensnared in the creamy cleavage.

"Uh-uh. Eyes up here, buddy."

There isn't any point in fighting the smile tugging at the corners of my mouth, but I take my time dragging my gaze up her chest, past those pouty lips, and finally locking onto that pissed-off scowl.

Virgin Mary Sweet has certainly turned into *all* woman.

Bet she tastes sweet, too.

"How about you stop ogling me and tell me your grand idea, Cass?"

"You come back to my place—"

"Oh, hell no. Do you think I'm going to fuck you for a candy cane? Like I'm some kind of candy cane ho? You mother—"

"Language, Miss Sweet, please."

We both turn to look at a grim-faced Old Jerry before he walks away, shaking his head in disgust.

"Yes, Miss Sweet, mind your tongue. There are children present." I mock an offended gasp of horror and draw my other hand up to clutch at my chest.

Anger clouds her pretty features. Pressing her buttons shouldn't be a turn-on, like foreplay, but somehow, it is. And if I manage to get her back to my place, there are so many things I want to do—with her *and* this candy cane.

Mary scans around us and pauses at a couple with

a toddler before turning her laser focus back to me. "Maybe you can talk *them* out of their candy, too." She tilts her head in the kid's direction.

I follow her gaze. *What the hell is she talking about?*

Mary catches me off guard and yanks her end of the candy cane toward her, trying to jerk it free while I'm distracted. I clench my jaw and pull it right back. She huffs an annoyed breath to blow the hair from her face. She purses her mouth, and a million different ideas for what Virgin Mary can do with those damn *lips* make my cock twitch.

But I need to get her alone first. "Before you so rudely interrupted me with your perversions, I was suggesting that we should go to my loft and split the candy cane."

Her golden eyes narrow on me with deep suspicion. "No tricks? We half it?"

I cross my fingers over my heart and hold up my hand with my thumb crossed over the palm. "Scout's honor."

She rolls her eyes hard enough that they almost don't come back down. "You weren't a scout, and that's not their sign."

Waving my hand at her, I scoff. "Close enough. Do we have a deal?" I flash her a dazzling smile, the one that always ensures big tips on the nights I work behind the bar.

Her lips pressed together firmly, she rolls her eyes yet again. "Fine. We'll half it."

Was that really so hard? Because God knows I am.

The satisfied grin taking over my lips only seems to make her sneer at me more. "Great. Let me just pay Old Jerry, and we'll get this bagged up and be on our way."

I reach for my wallet but feel a tug on the other end of the candy. My fingers brush against the leather of my wallet in my back pocket, and I meet Mary's glare.

"No way. I'm paying half. I want half ownership."

She can't be serious...

"Half ownership?" I stare at the deathly serious look on her face. "Mary, this is like a two-dollar piece of candy. I think I can afford to pay for the entire thing."

She shakes her head, sending her caramel silken locks shifting around her face, mesmerizing me. My fingers itch to dig into it and tug on it while she sucks *my* candy cane deep into that throat and laps at it with that tongue that can't seem to stop arguing with me.

"No,"—she squares her shoulders, a move that's probably intended to make her seem more intimidating, but all it does is push her luscious breasts toward me even more—"I'm paying for my half, but you're going to have to let it go so I can set down these bags and get the money out of my purse."

I look to her other hand, the one not latched onto the object of our argument. Her purse hangs from her elbow along with another bag of goods. "There's no way in hell I'm letting this go. You'll take off with it, claiming it all for yourself."

Her lips curl into a wicked smile. "You don't trust

me?" She bats her long, thick black lashes at me. What she thinks is mocking is truly sexy as hell.

"Not. Even. A. Little."

An animal-like growl rumbles in her chest, and she tightens her grip on the candy cane. "Sorry, Cass. I'm not letting go. I guess we'll stand here all day."

It's a battle of wills she won't win. I can stand here *all* day and do this. It wouldn't be the first time my hand was wrapped around ten inches for hours at a time—but when it's your own cock, at least you know there's a happy ending in sight. Sometimes even *I* have a dry spell, and a guy's gotta do what a guy's gotta do to get off.

Old Jerry sighs dramatically. I hadn't even noticed he had returned, but the annoyance twisting his wrinkled brow proves he's caught the gist of our current predicament. "Take the candy cane. Please, on the house. Take it and go. For the love of God, just go."

Mary plasters on a dazzling smile. "Jerry, thank you, but you don't have to do that." She practically coos the words at him, and I'm sure any other man would fall to their knees to worship at her feet, but he seems to be over our shit.

"Yes, I do. You're cursing and arguing are scaring off paying customers. I'm considering this a sacrificial candy cane." He waves a hand and wanders off, mumbling something under his breath about "crazy kids" and "strange ideas about phallic-shaped candies."

He has no idea.

Our gazes meet, and neither of us can contain our

laughter. The way it lights up her face and clears the anger from her eyes might almost convince me I have a chance with her, if she didn't also wrench hard on the candy in one final last-ditch effort to steal it from my grip.

"Well, we got a free candy cane out of it, but you need to let it go so I can carry it to my place. I have a loft over the bar. The walk isn't far." I pull on the source of our discontent.

Her jaw opens in disbelief. "*You* let go." She yanks on her end.

"Mary," I growl her name—her anger and persistence fueling my libido in a way that's left me borderline feral. I can't help but notice how she slightly shivers—my tone, the way my eyes rake across her features, and the suggestion I forced into her name—raising something to just below the surface of her pale skin. "I guess we're just going to walk to my place holding this, then, because I'm not letting go, either."

Mary chuckles. "Looks that way, *Casanova*." My name comes out as a smart-ass purr from those full lips, and my cock pushes against the seam of my zipper at her sass.

Down boy. Not the right place or the right time for that notion.

"Well, grip it tightly, Virgin Mary. Cass is going to take you for a ride."

Blush colors her cheeks, and I hide my grin behind my hand before I turn and lead her through the market toward the sidewalk that will carry us the short distance down to my loft.

Neither one of us is willing to release our phallic prize. Only the length of the candy separates us, and this close, the light breeze blows that sweet and fruity scent from her hair straight into the air I breathe.

"You sure you don't want to let go?" I sneak a glance at her out of the corner of my eye.

She doesn't even look at me, just struts with her head held high, perfect tits pushed out. "Not a chance."

We stroll down the sidewalk, hands linked via massive dick-shaped candy. It's utterly ridiculous, but I can't help the chuckle that escapes me as we pass a few people on the sidewalk. The odd sight draws curious stares.

Mary leans forward slightly until our gazes meet. "What? What's so funny?"

She seems either unaware or unconcerned with how completely stupid we must look right now.

"Nothing, Virgin Mary. We're here." I stop outside the door to my bar.

She glances at it. I need to wrangle my keys out of my pocket to unlock the stairwell door, but Mary still has a kung-fu grip on this damn candy cane. She returns her focus to me, a scowl turning down her lips. "Stop calling me that."

I bite back the laugh at her annoyance over the old nickname. It's just so much fun to get her riled up. "Mary, I need to get to my keys. Let go. I'll let you hold something else in its place that's big, long, and hard."

Her jaw drops, but it's almost as if I've rendered her speechless. And caught her off-guard.

This is my chance.

I jerk the treasure out of her hand and lean in close enough that I know she feels my warm breath fluttering over her cheek. "You better close that sweet mouth, Virgin Mary, or that big, long, hard thing is going to slip right in there."

Chapter Three

MARY

Each step we climb up wooden stairs brings us closer to a landing with a single door in front. It also draws my attention to the fact that Cass still has an absolutely incredible ass. The man always did have an amazing body. But he was a teenager back then, had a high metabolism and played baseball. A huge part of me had wished if I ran into him, he would have totally let himself go and gone all "dad bod."

No such luck.

Instead, his jeans perfectly hug a tight ass positioned directly in front of my face. It might have been wise to go up ahead of him so I wouldn't find myself in this predicament, but after that *lewd* comment he made before he unlocked the door, I didn't want him anywhere near *my* ass. Something tells me if I had ascended in front of him, his hands would have been all over my globes, and that would have led to exactly what he threatened—something big, long, and hard in my hand or mouth—and definitely *not* the candy cane.

A girl can only take so much shameless flirting from a super-hot guy she's fantasized about for years before she finally snaps. And I'm not too far from the brink of that.

Only I know he does this with *everyone*—exhibit A—mom with a baby at the market.

Don't take anything he says seriously, Mare. If you do, you'll only set yourself up for disappointment and rejection, even worse than what he did to you a decade ago.

He pauses on the landing and slips the key into the lock. His azure eyes peek over his shoulder at me before he unlocks the door and pushes it open.

I can only imagine the frat-house-style décor I'm about to be greeted with since Cass lives over a bar. There will probably be neon signs and beer bongs all over the place. Though from the quick glimpse I got of the bar downstairs, it didn't look *too* trashy.

In fact, it almost looked—I can't believe this is the word that comes to mind with *anything* having to do with Cass—classy. He's somehow managed to carve out a thriving business in our tiny little hometown.

The bastard.

It would have made me feel so much better if he were a deadbeat loser.

"After you." The hand not holding the candy cane sweeps out, granting me entrance.

A clean, crisp scent mingled with new leather greets me.

Wow. I was definitely not expecting...THIS.

No mere bachelor pad with hand-me-down furniture—it's masculine and beautiful. Absolutely stunning, really.

Slate floors grace the entire open living area. An enormous matching fireplace, two-stories high, flanked by built-in shelves lined with books and photos, takes up one entire wall, and the leather couch and armchair facing it make the space inviting and cozy.

A wall of windows to my left frames a beautiful, real Christmas tree and overlooks the town square with an unobstructed view of the old courthouse in all its eighteenth-century charm.

I bet this view is beautiful at night.

"This is your place?" My eyes turn toward the kitchen, with beautiful cabinetry and a massive stainless-steel island littered with perfectly placed bottles of booze and mixers on either side of a seamless sink so large it could be considered a small bathtub.

This must be where he perfects his drinks.

"Try not to look so shocked, Mary. Were you expecting it to look like a frat house?"

Yes. Yes, I was.

Except I don't say that. I don't say anything. Probably safer that way. Instead, I focus on the source of all our angst today, still clutched tightly in his large hand.

"Ready to enjoy this bad boy?" He wiggles it in front of his crotch playfully.

My throat suddenly goes dry, and I force myself to drag my eyes up to finally meet his. He offers a knowing, smug grin and an obnoxious wink. Butterflies swirl low in my belly, and my skin heats. My body still wants Cass A. Nova despite my head telling me he's still a jerk, but I shove that shit away.

Just old feelings from a lifetime ago. Hormones and my cobweb-filled vagina calling out to be occupied.

Forget it, Mare.

We both kick off our boots, and reluctantly, I follow him into the kitchen, keeping my eyes on the room and not his amazing ass. He drapes his jacket over the back a stool and heads directly for the sink, and I set my bags onto the island and watch him like a hawk. I don't trust the man not to do something underhanded in order to keep the full length of that peppermint treat. If you give him an inch, he'll take a mile. And my career here in town, the restaurant, all depend on this party going off without a hitch.

Don't let Cass A. Nova be a hitch!

He sets the candy cane on the counter and flips on the water, the sound of it pouring into the metal sink filling the tension-filled silence. Strong fingers glide back and forth as he washes his hands, and I can't help but imagine a naked, wet Cass stoking himself and touching me with those hands. Which is likely exactly what he intended with the move. But even knowing that doesn't stop the visual from assaulting me.

Get yourself together, Mary.

Dragging my focus away from his slow, deliberate

movements takes more willpower than I ever could have thought, but I somehow manage to meet his eyes. Of course, the asshole is watching me, and a knowing smirk tugs at his lips. His full, kissable lips.

I choke back a moan at the intensity of that smoldering gaze raking over me. This pull between us...I can't be the only one feeling it.

Can I?

It's the same feeling I got every time he looked at me growing up, only then, when he directed his focus on me, it wasn't with this kind of heat. Whatever it might be now, I need to move the hell on from it. Unfortunately, I know from experience a one-sided thing for this man doesn't work out in my favor.

Been there. Done that. Have the emotional scars that will never fade.

He examines me from under thick lashes before his gaze darts back to the task at hand.

Christ, I bet he knows what he's doing to me...

I nervously tug at the collar of my sweater before I pull off my jacket and lay it across a stool beside me at the island. This is what he wanted, to get me hot and bothered, and I bet that man has a massive dick. He's too cocky not to be well endowed. Plus, what I could make out under all his tight baseball pants and wet swim trunks as a teenager has remained seared in my mind like a damn brand with the initials C.A.N. on it.

Squirming on the stool under me, I try to find a position that might stop the throbbing between my legs. No such luck. My body seems to want what my head knows I can't have. I can't be fooled by good looks and innuendos. It may have been ten years since I last saw Cass, but I still know who he is—what he is. While he's a good person—and hot as all get out—he's also a huge flirt. Always has been. With *everyone.*

Well, everyone except me. Before today…

Being in the proximity of Cass is dangerous. Instead of ogling him and fantasizing more, I force myself to rise and walk deliberately over toward the bookshelves so it doesn't look like I'm running away. Which I *totally* am.

The worn leather spines of several classic novels call out to me, and I brush my fingertips over them with awe.

Who would have thought Cass was a reader?

Growing up, the only thing I ever saw Cass and Bobby reading was a secret stash of girly magazines. It's hard to believe his tastes ever improved.

The water shuts off behind me, and I peek over my shoulder at the kitchen. Cass leans casually against the counter, just watching me inspect his things. I arch a brow but turn my attention back to his shelves. Nothing good can come from lingering stares at this man.

A photo of Cass and a group of boys all decked out in matching baseball uniforms holds the place of honor in the center of one shelf. They raise a trophy in triumph and have the number one held up with their fingers. Each face proud and happy. No one looks happier than Cass.

It's so sweet and endearing that he helps them. It makes me sick. I can't reconcile the Cass I knew so many years ago with the man he seems to be now.

Especially when I glance to where he still leans against the counter, watching me, entirely unaffected.

Just like all those years ago when he was the center of my small world and I was nothing but the punchline of a joke to him.

I return my attention to the shelves and make my way down the line of photos. Cass and Bobby at the restaurant's grand opening. Cass and his parents in front of a Christmas tree. Cass and...

Shit.

The woman and the baby from the market earlier. Cass with his arm wrapped tightly around her shoulders as she leans in to him. Matching smiles on their faces while they look down to the child cradled in her arms.

My heart sinks. Bile climbs its way up my throat, threatening to make an appearance.

He's married! Or at the very least, romantically involved with her...and a father.

"Are you jealous?" His whispered words are so close, they send chills skittering down my spine and make me jump.

I jerk away and snort in derision. "Don't be absurd. Why would I be jealous?"

Definitely not jealous. More like I feel like a total fool.

Here I've been ogling someone who is clearly taken

by someone who might have seen us together at the market.

Oh, God...this is so bad. I need to get what I came for and go.

Cass brushes his fingertips lightly along the back of my arm, raising goosebumps in their wake. "That's Kaitlyn, my sister, and my niece, Daniella. They just moved back to town a few months ago."

A little sigh of relief slips from my lips. I hadn't even recognized her. Between the weight loss and lack of the signature thick black glasses she used to wear, I never would have believed it was little Kaitlyn Nova. The last decade really changed her.

Thank God I'm not fantasizing about a taken man.

His warm breath flutters against the back of my neck. "I saw how you used to stare at me when I was in my baseball uniform. You liked what you saw. In fact, Sweet Mary, I believe that you still do." He brushes his lips against the shell of my ear and presses the length of his warm, hard body into my back.

Move, stupid!

But I'm paralyzed by the curl of sensuality lacing his words. It renders me speechless and immobile. If I shift even slightly, my knees might give out, and I can't let him see my weakness. With concentrated effort, I push my way through the haze and turn to face him.

Big mistake.

He's gorgeous, arrogant, and oh, so sure of himself —swagger for days held in that grin. And he's only inches away from me, so close the heat of his body radiates between the tiny gap between us. He takes a step forward, brushing his chest against mine.

My nipples immediately pebble at the contact, and I shove at his chest, trying to give myself some space to break this spell. "You're so full of yourself. Stop being mean."

But I can't deny the truth in his words.

God, did I ogle him.

Something flickers in his Caribbean-blue eyes—almost like he understands something for the first time, and he captures my face in his palm. "I'm not being mean, Mary. I'm teasing you because I like you." His voice drops an octave, like a lover whispering secret promises against silken sheets.

My toes curl with anticipation of what he'll say next.

He glides his free hand back around my shoulder. "Didn't anyone ever tell you in elementary school that the boys who pick on you and tug your hair do it as an expression of affection?"

His fingers twine into my locks and pull, while a panty-wetting smile spreads across his lips.

My breath catches, my lungs unwilling or unable to work when every inhalation only sucks in his scent—denim and crisply fallen snow.

Holy shit! Is Cass flirting with me? Really flirting with me?

Cass brushes his thumb across my cheek slowly. "You were always cute, Mary, but you were my best friend's kid sister and far too young to ever handle the kind of guy I was back then. Plus, I was sort of an asshole."

His confession doesn't help me find my breath. In fact, I have to consciously inhale deeply before the room starts spinning from a lack of oxygen.

All those years, I dreamed of this moment, of being in the arms of Cass A. Nova. Of having him say these words to me.

And now, it's all happening because of a candy cane.

The absurdity of this situation rips a laugh from somewhere deep in my chest. "You're still an asshole."

Stepping inexplicably closer, Cass tugs at the ends of my hair again. His lips hover mere millimeters from mine. The endless-blue depths of his eyes swirl with waves of lust and need and something even more wicked. "Yeah, but you like it."

Chapter Four

CASS

Mary's perfect-pink lips curl into a soft smile, but it doesn't hide her nervousness. The quiver in her voice gives her away. I stroke my thumb across her bottom lip, and she slowly shuts her eyes, an exhale of warm breath gliding across my palm.

She leans into my touch, just the slightest acknowledgment that she's on-board, but it's all the invitation I need to take what I've wanted since the moment I looked up to see who held the other end of that candy cane.

I close the minuscule distance between us, sealing my mouth to hers. The soft flesh yields under the pressure of my kiss, and I finally get my first taste of her, not even bothering to bite back the groan that rumbles in my chest.

Sweet fuck...if I had known it could be like this with Mary, I might not have waited so damn long.

I twine my fingers into her hair tighter, half growling and deepening the kiss. Something sweet and comforting like cinnamon dances from her tongue to mine and the heat of sunshine seems to radiate from her into me, warming me from the inside out. I pull her curvy frame closer to me and slide my other hand around her waist.

She breaks our kiss, a giggle bubbling from between the lips I just had pressed against mine.

"What's so funny?" My voice comes out raspy and full of need. It's almost embarrassing how desperate I am to have my mouth back on hers.

Her gaze drops to my straining erection encased in my jeans, and her laughter brings tears to her eyes. If I weren't so confident in my manhood, I might be offended. But I still don't get what's so damn funny.

She finally manages to contain her hysterics long enough to inhale a sharp breath and meet my eyes with humor in hers. "Is that a candy cane in your pocket, or are you just happy to see me?"

I bark out a laugh that echoes around my place, bouncing off the slate floors, but then she pulls back and narrows a scrutinizing look at me, the lightness of the moment suddenly gone in an instant.

"Is this all a ploy to steal away the candy cane for yourself?"

"Well, that *wasn't* my plan, but now that you mention it..." I scoop her up, eliciting a squeal of surprise.

"Cass, what are you doing?"

Instead of answering her, I crush my lips to hers, and she wraps her arms around my neck before twining her fingers into my hair. Her tongue brushes mine, and our kiss turns frantic.

Something I don't dare acknowledge courses through my veins, mixing with the lust and desire that's bubbled beneath my skin since the moment she walked back into my life.

I'm making out with Virgin Mary. And if the shit she's doing with her tongue is any indication, she's not a virgin anymore.

Thank fuck for that.

Because what I have planned might be a bit much for a shy, innocent virgin like she was all those years ago.

I drag my mouth away from hers to stalk to the kitchen and set her onto the island, but she's back on me in the blink of an eye. And I'm right there with her.

This is *not* the Virgin Mary Sweet I grew up with. This is Mary Sweet unleashed. And it is so damn fucking hot.

Her frantic hands tug at the hem of my sweater. "Sweater off. Now."

I'm all too happy to obey her command. We have far too many clothes on, and while I'd rather be undressing her first, it won't be long until I expose every single inch of her flawless, creamy skin.

I grab the collar of my sweater behind my neck and yank the material over my head with one hand, letting it fall to the floor wherever it may.

"Holy shit! You're still hot!" Mary's tongue darts out to wet her lips, and she runs her hands down my abs.

I clench the muscles there to make them stand out more. She issues a low throaty moan of approval and trails a leisurely finger down the *V* that runs into the waistband of my jeans. I let my eyes drift closed, my cock so hard it's almost painful. All it wants is to be buried deep inside her, but I have something even more fun in mind for Mary.

Taking her face in my hands, I kiss her again, slowly and softly this time. "No mojitos, no cake. Our customers will just have to do without anything candy cane tonight because I have other plans for it. Very, dirty fucking plans, Sweet Mary."

Her eyes widen slightly—a mix of shock and confusion darkening them—before a tiny gasp slips from her lips as she apparently comprehends just where my thoughts about her and this peppermint rod are headed.

She offers me a knowing smile, and I lean back in, pushing her down onto the cool surface of the island with my warm body.

"You're fucking dirty, Cass."

I grin at her and waggle my eyebrows playfully. "Fuck, yes I am." I pin her arms above her head and drop my mouth to hers for another searing kiss before I pull away and waggle my eyebrows. "And you fucking love it."

She doesn't protest, just giggles, and I lean in to nip her lips and twirl our tongues, relentlessly exploring.

My cock twitches in anticipation, and I release my grip on her arms and trace a path down her sides to grasp the soft material of the hem of her sweater. I break our kiss only to pull the fabric up and over her head, tossing it to the floor without care.

With what I have in mind, we won't be needing clothes for a *long* time.

I let my gaze drift to her perfect tits encased in soft purple lace. "Mary..." Her name comes out a half-feral growl. My body practically vibrates to unwrap the rest of her.

Mary Sweet naked and under me...

Who would have thought I'd be so close?

I push down the lacy cups of her lingerie, baring her perfect tits to me. Her nipples harden to high peaks, begging me to drop my head for a taste. My mouth waters. My heartbeat pulses through my cock, and I swirl my tongue around one of her raised points, drawing a moan of approval from Mary. But I don't linger long, shifting my focus to her other breast.

She reaches out and claws for purchase amid my oral assault, but her hands only rattle the bottles of liquor and mixers resting on the island from my last cocktail experiment.

The honey pot draws my eye, sparking another idea.

I hope Mary is on board.

After one more quick suck on her nipple, I let it free from my lips with a *pop* and grab the honey.

Mary's gaze follows my hand as I remove the lid and grip the wooden spoon.

"Cass?"

In answer, I stroke a finger over her nipple before gently applying pressure, making her arch up for more.

Oh, I am going to give her so much more.

I lift the wooden spoon and hover it over the taut peak, watching enraptured as the golden substance slowly drips across her creamy flesh.

"Fuck." The word slips out on a whisper of awe, but I waste no time lapping up the sweet goodness.

Mary's hands clutch at my hair, holding me to her while I lap at her sweet, delicate flesh. "Cass—"

A strangled moan slipping from her lips cuts off whatever else she was going to say, and it serves to kick me into high gear. Leaning back, I swiftly move to the button of her jeans.

I tap her hips. "Raise up. Let me get these off."

She complies by lifting her ass off the island so I can peel her tight jeans and purple panties off in one smooth glide, letting my fingers drag along her legs, leaving goose bumps across her pale skin.

"Damn, Mary." Her pussy glistens in the light streaming in from the windows overlooking the street and the twinkling multi-colored lights from my tree, and my tongue darts out across my lips in anticipation of finally tasting her.

I spread her legs open wide, and she twines her fingers into my hair, giving it a gentle tug of encouragement.

Like I need any to do this...

This woman is so beautiful. So damn *sexy*. And she isn't even trying to be. She's just being...Mary. All that arguing only served to build up the tension between us and make me desperate to take everything from her, at least, everything she's willing to offer.

I languidly lick from bottom to top, flicking my tongue over her clit until her nails dig into my scalp. She writhes under me, rolling her hips up against my face. Her arousal coats my tongue.

Good. I need her absolutely soaked and panting for what I have planned.

More than that...

I need her *desperate.*

She's so wet now that I easily slide two fingers inside her while I suck on her sensitive bundle of nerves, driving her higher.

"Shit! Shit! Shit!" Her chant echoes around the loft, ringing in my ears and making my cock ache to be inside her. "Cass, more! God, I need more!"

The urgency in her tone brings a chuckle up my throat to vibrate against her wet skin. I feel it, too. This need. This knowledge that I will never get too much of Mary Sweet.

I use my free hand to unbutton my own pants without stopping. Something tells me if I did, Mary would lash out at me with a litany of curse words that would prove she's not the sweet virgin she was back when she had a crush on me. Yanking my pants from my hips one-handed finally allows my cock to spring free, a welcome reprieve from the tight confinement it's been straining against.

Mary's lust-soaked eyes bore into me, watching my every move, and I reluctantly pull my mouth from her clit and my fingers from Mary's clenching pussy to stand to my full height.

Her gaze devours me the way I just did her, and I bite my lip and stroke my shaft slowly.

Fuck, that feels good.

Not as good as it will feel to be inside her, though. Something tells me nothing will.

I tap her thigh with my free hand. "Put your feet on the counter, Mary. Spread your legs wide. Let me look at you."

She leans back onto her elbows and does as I ask, and when I look down, my cock jumps with appreciation. Mary is no longer that awkward little sister of my best friend. She's all fucking woman. Every beautiful, curvy inch of her.

Every inch I want to defile.

I grab the sweet treat that brought us to this moment, and I've never been more eager to hold a sugary confection in my hand. With its length and girth, it was practically designed for this type of depravity. I rip the wrapper from it and bring it between her legs. Mary giggles, and I look up to meet her gaze with a devious grin.

She raises a slender eyebrow playfully. "Is that candy cane disease-free?"

I bark out a laugh at the clear comparison between

this phallic piece of candy and my dick and the obvious question in it.

Am I clean?

"Yeah." I wiggle the swirled peppermint stick lasciviously. "It's been tested. And it hasn't left the candy store in six months."

Mary's lips tilt into a smirk. "Good to know Cass A. Nova. My lady garden hasn't been watered in about a year."

A year? If this woman was anywhere near me during that time, I would have made sure she was never in a sexual drought. Her garden would have been drenched daily. Multiple times.

"So, no condom, then?" I nudge the end of the candy cane against her wet flesh and grin.

Please say yes.

Mary bareback will be like finding Heaven. I'm confident of that.

She laughs and nods her agreement. "I'm on the pill."

That is music to my ears.

Focusing on the task at hand, I swirl the smooth, silken candy lightly against her clit.

"Shit! It's cold!" She shrieks and smacks her hands against the counter, jerking her legs closed while our laughter mingles.

I spread apart her legs again with my forearms. "It won't be for long."

Not if I have my way. I apply a little extra pressure

against her sensitive bundle of nerves. She moans her approval, and her legs fall farther apart.

"Fuck, Mary." I can't seem to drag my gaze from her pussy, watching transfixed as I trail the sweet stick down to her opening and gently push just the tip inside.

"Mmm, Cass." Her fingers meet her clit and begin to move in lazy, unhurried circles while I work more of the candy cane in and out of her.

It doesn't take but a second for us to find a rhythm, but I can't stand it much longer. Seeing this phallic sweet in the place I so badly want to be is pure torture. I knock her hand out of the way and suck her clit into my mouth while I continue to fuck her tight cunt with the holiday treat that brought us together and work my rigid shaft with my other hand.

Sweet fuck!

It's raunchy and lewd and *oh so wrong,* but I don't want it to stop. Our mingled moans of pleasure only serve to turn me on more. Mary finally finds her release, her hot pussy clenching around the pseudo-cock hard enough to almost tug it from my grip. Her head falls back on a moan, and I keep stroking myself and gently pull out the candy cane while she recovers.

Her laugh breaks through the sound of our panting breaths, and her eyes reach mine. Mary Sweet is the most beautiful woman I have *ever* seen. Legs spread wide, waiting for more. Ready and waiting for *me.*

And I'm not about to make her wait any longer. Because Christ knows, I sure as hell can't.

I smile at all the dirty thoughts that spring to my mind about all the ways I plan on making this woman come. My cock strains to get inside her, and I keep stroking it and bring the stick to my mouth and take long, slow licks from the end that was just shoved inside her. The flavor that is all Mary and sweet peppermint bursts along my tongue, and I growl deep in my chest at her taste and the contentment it spreads through my body.

Mary watches, licking her lips, and I hold our "toy" out to her. She leans forward slowly and wraps her lips around it seductively, gliding down the length slightly before she sucks hard. Her eyes drift closed, and she issues a low moan of approval, relishing in the naughtiness that just transpired between us as much as I am.

"Knowing that just made you come..." I shake my head, words escaping me. "That is the hottest thing I've ever seen."

I pull it from her mouth and toss the candy cane onto the island beside her, crashing my lips to hers while I align my cock with her opening. Our kiss is a minty hot, searing brand, the taste of her pussy and the crisp, clean candy rolling on our tongues as I finally guide myself inside Mary's velvety-smooth, perfect cunt.

Chapter Five

MARY

Cass has every right to be cocky—he is a sexual god.

Never, in all of my fantasies, did I think this would be the reality of being with him. I'm already on the verge of another orgasm, and he must sense it because he glides a hand between us to apply pressure to my clit.

He pounds into me, his cock bringing me sweet oblivion while stars dance on the edge of my vision.

"Cass. I'm going to come." I manage to force the words from my lips between pants. "God, oh, God!"

"Come on my cock, Mary." He whispers the words into my ear then gently takes a playful nip of my lobe.

I roll my hips up to meet him. He impales me over and over again, and I chant his name in time with his thrusts until I finally fall over the edge.

His strokes turn lazy and long, and I scratch my nails up the length of his back, riding out my orgasm. I tighten my legs around his waist, digging my heels into his lower back, and it changes the angle slightly, dragging the head of his cock along that elusive spot deep inside of me.

It begins a whole new ascent. Drawing me toward another orgasm, I'm not sure I can handle. His panting breaths at my ear drive me insane. It's sensory overload. The room spins, and my vision blurs. A lust-soaked haze hovers in my head.

He moves, sliding his arms under my back to draw me closer so he can quicken his pace again. I'm nothing more than a boneless, panting mess in his arms. A stream of cusswords falls mindlessly past my lips, and I hang on for my very life while the literal man of my dreams rides me to the edge of another orgasm.

"Cass, I can't, I can't take it. It's too much," I practically beg him, but if he stopped, I'm confident I would cry and possibly die on the spot.

"Yes." Thrust. *"You."* Thrust. *"Can."* Thrust. Each word marked by a deep stroke drives home his confidence in me.

A cacophony of sensations overrides my ability to speak again, and I hurtle into bliss. This man—candy cane fornicator, vagina conqueror, king of orgasms, and dry-spell curse breaker—is bringing his A-game.

His hands slide out from under me and grab at my legs, untangling me from around him. I whine in protest, but he ignores me and grabs for the honey again.

Holy shit.

He drizzles the golden, sweet syrup on my pussy and tosses the wooden spoon before he dives in. His tongue licks a trail from my ass all the way up to my clit, where he issues a deep, rumbling groan that might as well be a vibrator against my overly stimulated skin.

Thank God I kept up with my waxing appointments even through my year-long dry spell.

He nibbles my sensitive flesh, and by the time I finally come on his tongue, I'm nearly hyperventilating. He pushes my legs apart, licking every drop of my release from my body, dragging out the pleasure and overwhelming my senses...yet again.

"Mary." My name falls from his lips, a feather-light whisper, almost a prayer, the word ghosting across my flesh.

I shiver at the unfamiliar feeling his awed voice stirs within me, but I don't have long to think about what it could be because my gaze follows Cass reaching a hand for the candy cane.

Oh, God...not again. I don't know if I can take it.

He runs the end of the candy up the seam between my legs. The coolness of it against my over-heated, sticky flesh sends goose bumps scattering everywhere. He slips it inside slowly.

Cass leans down and stops with his lips a mere hair's breadth from mine. "I could fuck you all day."

I don't doubt his words or his stamina. This man does not lack in that department...or, hell, any. I drink him in with open covetousness—from his beautiful eyes focused on fucking me with the thick rod to his gorgeous face, complete with angular jawline graced with stubble. My gaze drifts down his muscled neck, and my mouth waters to bite it as soon as possible before my eyes track to the hard, muscled pecs dusted with light-colored hair. His six-pack bulges and shifts with his every move, driving the candy cane in and out of me with increasing speed and laser-focused precision.

His bicep bulges every time his clenched fist strokes his hard shaft. I hum my approval and suck in a deep breath. This man is an Adonis, and I can truly appreciate the time he must put in at the gym to maintain his physique.

I want every hard inch of him pushed against me, inside of me, all over me. Reaching between us, I yank the candy from between my legs and from his hand.

His gaze darts up to meet mine. "What's wrong? Are you okay?"

The look of concern in his eyes and marring his brows undoes me. He'd stop right now if I asked him to and wouldn't even be worried about his thick, unsatisfied hard-on that juts out between us. That thought only makes me hornier.

I hold the candy cane out toward his mouth, and his eyes stay trained on mine while he leans forward and licks where it's covered in my release. He closes his eyes, almost as if he's savoring my essence. Then his tongue darts out and across his lips, and when the muscles of his throat move as he swallows, I snap. I drag him toward me by his muscular arms and slam my mouth to his in a claiming, searing kiss.

Years of wanting Cass since we were teens and now as a full-grown, beautiful man pour from me, and I give it all to him in my kiss. Every day I waited in vain for him to see me as more than Bobby's kid sister. Every time I looked at him with little-girl love in my eyes. But now, I'm a grown woman, and he finally sees me as such for the first time...and it undoes me.

I reach between us, my fingers unable to meet around the width of him. Twining my tongue with his, I line up his cock with my pussy. He digs his hands into my hips, lifting me from the counter. I tighten my legs around him, and he bounces up into me, impaling me on his impossibly hard length.

Ecstasy like I've never known roars through my veins, demanding my release as he pushes, harder and faster, and we both fight, reaching for that ultimate release.

My breath stalls in my lungs. My heart thuds against my chest so hard, it feels as though it might burst from it. Yet Cass keeps barreling me toward the edge. I angle my head down to the spot where his neck meets his shoulder and bite down as yet another orgasm assaults my senses. He groans and jerks within the cage of my arms, blasting out his own release.

He lowers me to the counter again. His fingers grip the hair at the nape of my neck and tug silently, asking me to look up at him.

Christ...

I hesitate slightly. My brother's best friend just fucked me stupid. With a candy cane and his dick. My chest tightens, and I avoid his gaze. This must be the "after" awkwardness I was too horny to be concerned about earlier.

Gentle, warm fingers trace down my spine, and I slowly release my teeth from the flesh on his neck where he will no doubt have a mark. But I can't look at him yet; instead, I focus on that burgundy spot my mouth left and feel a little tug somewhere deep in my gut.

At least that shows me this was real. It happened. After all of these years of pining after Cass, having my heart broken by his rejection, he's now stuck with an undeniable piece of me. No matter how temporary it may be.

"Mary, look at me."

I close my eyes and inhale one last deep breath, preparing myself for the fall out of what just transpired between us. When it finally feels like I may have regained some semblance of control over myself and my body, I raise my head fully and open my eyes. His lock with mine, and my heart stutters at how beautiful this man is.

"That was... intense." He laughs, his fingers mindlessly twirling a curl of my hair above my rushing heart.

I smile and try to push down old feelings flooding my system. "Yeah."

Only mere moments ago, it felt like I was owning him, rocking his world, yet now, it's like I'm back to being fourteen, lusting after Cass A. Nova, wanting something unattainable. Just out of my reach.

But even if I can never have him again, I can't regret this. Not even a little bit. This baggage is mine to pull along. Cass didn't make any grand promises. There may not be more than this one bright moment between us, and I refuse to tarnish it with what-ifs.

"What's going on in that pretty head of yours, Mary? Where'd you go?"

Down a path best left untraveled.

But I don't say that. Instead, my mind jumps back to here, now, the food I have to make for Becky's party soon and the fact that I no longer have the ingredient I need to make her day complete.

"Shit. The cake! The event! I need to go! How am I going to explain the lack of this cake to the hostess from hell?"

I am so, so screwed. And not just because Cass has his still-hard dick buried inside me.

"Mary, it will be okay—"

"How? What can I even say to her? *'Sorry about the cake you wanted, Becky. The one item that you insisted upon. You see, I found the perfect candy cane, but my childhood crush was attached to the other end. One thing led to another, then I let a man named Cass A. Nova fuck me with it before he banged me senseless with his massive cock.'*" I shake my head and laugh at myself.

Dear Lord, I let him fuck me with a candy cane.

I push at his chest until he releases a sigh and takes

a tiny step back, his dick slipping from inside me. Biting back a groan at the loss, I weasel out from around him and begin the search for my clothes.

Which are apparently strewn all over the loft. Every time I bend down to pick up a piece of clothing, his eyes follow me. They sear my skin the same way he did my heart when he was inside me.

Why does this have to be so damn awkward? Way to ho, Mare. Fucking everything up, aren't you?

I slip into my bra and reach back to clasp it, but a large hand wraps around mine and pushes it out of the way to complete the task. He tugs on my shoulder to turn me toward him, and a firm hand lifts my chin. My eyes meet his, and I sigh. Literally sigh, as I'm struck by his hotness.

Why does he have to be so damn gorgeous?

Concern dances in his eyes, and he brushes his thumb across my cheek. "I'll come with you. I'll talk to Becky and offer free bar service for her party to appease her."

"What?" I shake my head. "Cass, this is no small party. That's a lot of booze. Why would you do that for me?"

His thumb brushes my bottom lip as he considers my question. "I don't want you to be placed in a bad position with a client because our sex got a little...creative." He smiles down at me—still hot, still naked as fuck—but it's full of warmth and sincerity. "But..."

Of course, there's a but.

"You come back here after the party tonight. I want

to spend more time with you. I'd like to get to know you, who you are now. Not Virgin Mary, but Sweet-Ass Mary, who drives me literally insane in the best way. Deal?"

What?

I open my mouth and close it, trying to figure out how to respond to his demand. "You want to see me again? I figured this was a one-and-done type of deal."

He shakes his head, a wicked grin on his all-too-perfect lips. "Sorry, Mary. I didn't get enough of you. Not sure that I can. Now, if you're in agreement with my terms, let's take a shower, get you cleaned up. Plus, I might need to fuck you once more before we get ready for this party. What do you say?"

"What about the bar? Don't you need to be there tonight?"

He leans in and brushes a tender kiss across my lips. "I have employees who can handle it. I'll just have to warn them about the lack of candy cane for the mojitos. Now, *what do you say? Do we have a deal?*"

Hell yeah!

Except I don't say that. That would sound too much like fourteen-year-old Virgin Mary being a giddy schoolgirl in front of her crush. Instead, I swallow thickly and try to appear non-affected by the fact that he's pressing his hardening cock against my stomach.

"Yeah. I guess I'm okay with those terms." I smile and bat my lashes innocently.

Cass catches me off guard and snatches me up, cradling me in his arms. "You guess? What do you mean, *you guess?*" His soft lips land on mine, bringing a smile I can't fight. "Let's get you cleaned up so I can dirty you up all over again."

A contented sigh slips past my lips. I'm not sure where this is headed or what could be there between us long-term. But it's definitely something I'm willing to explore with Cass.

I haven't felt this way in a long time, or well, since the *first time* all those years ago when I tried to give my heart to this handsome man, my candy cane lover. This time, it seems like he's more than willing to take it.

We hope you enjoyed this spicy holiday treat!

For another steamy story from Gwyn and Christy, check out *Royally Complicated*, our super spicy bad boy royal/good girl commoner romance: books2read.com/RoyallyComplicated

To stay up to date on releases from Gwyn and Christy, sign up for Gwyn's newsletter here: www.gwynmcnamee.com/newsletter

ABOUT THE AUTHORS

Gwyn McNamee is an attorney, writer, wife, and mother (to one human baby and one fur baby). Originally from the Midwest, Gwyn relocated to her husband's home town of Las Vegas in 2015 and is enjoying her respite from the cold and snow. Gwyn loves to write stories with a bit of suspense and action mingled with romance and heat. When she isn't either writing or voraciously devouring any books she can get her hands on, Gwyn is busy adding to her tattoo collection, golfing, and stirring up trouble with her perfect mix of sweetness and sarcasm (usually while wearing heels). Gwyn loves to hear from her readers, and here's where you can find her:

Newsletter: www.gwynmcnamee.com/newsletter
Website: http://www.gwynmcnamee.com/
FB Reader Group: bit.ly/GwynMcNameeRG
Facebook: bit.ly/GwynMcNameeFB
Tiktok: bit.ly/TikTokGM

ABOUT THE AUTHORS

Instagram: bit.ly/GwynMcNameeIG
Twitter: bit.ly/GwynMcNameeTwitter
Goodreads: bit.ly/GwynMcNameeGR
Bookbub: bit.ly/GwynMcNameeBB

Writing with a whole lot of sarcasm and humor, mixed with a bit of Southern charm, Christy Anderson ain't no sweet tea kinda storyteller. As an author of romance, Christy believes it doesn't always have to be hearts and flowers; sometimes, it is dark and twisted, but romance nonetheless. She mixes terror, revenge, and a sliver of love and hope into stories about family, friends, struggles, blurred lines, and happily-ever-afters. Christy lives in the beautiful mountains of Eastern Tennessee with her husband and 152 cats (not really, but close), where she enjoys writing one twist at a time. Christy loves to hear from her readers, and here's where you can find her:

Newsletter: https://www.christyanderson.net/newsletter
Website: https://www.christyanderson.net/
Christy's Little Birds: bit.ly/ChristysReaderGroup
Facebook: bit.ly/ChristyAndersonFB
Instagram: bit.ly/ChristyAndersonInstagram
Goodreads: bit.ly/ChristyAndersonGoodreads
BookBub: bit.ly/ChristyAndersonBookBub

Printed in Great Britain
by Amazon